Caroline Maximus Hankinson is a nature and animal enthusiast, driven to write after the birth of her daughter, Belle-Valentina. Suddenly, her surroundings were through the eyes of a child. Being an owner of three ponies, four dogs and two goats, she incorporated the characters of her animals into her stories. Residing in a quaint cottage in rural Wiltshire, her bright, beautiful fairy-tale like garden decor depicts her broad appreciation for a world of imagination. Her stories are a reflection of the morals that she hopes to instil in her daughter throughout her life.

CAROLINE MAXIMUS HANKINSON

BIG HORNS LITTLE HORNS

AUSTIN MACAULEY PUBLISHERS®
LONDON • CAMBRIDGE • NEW YORK • SHARJAH

A CIP catalogue record for this title is available from the British Library.

ISBN 9781035800063 (Paperback)

ISBN 9781035800056 (Hardback)

ISBN 9781035800070 (ePub e-book)

www.austinmacauley.com

First Published 2025

Austin Macauley Publishers Ltd®

1 Canada Square

Canary Wharf

London

E14 5AA

Thank you to my parents, Michael and Christine Hankinson, for their love and support throughout my life and to all my friends for always believing in me. And not to forget all my animals for their constant source of unconditional love and entertainment. Also, to my daughter Belle-Valentina for bringing a powerful sense of motivation into my life.

Thank you to Austin Macauley Publishers for believing in my writing and for their support during its publication.

As they stood there grazing,

Edward Chocolate's big horns looked amazing.

Edward Chocolate was always winning a fight.

Whilst Bertie Boo Boo thought, *this just isn't right.*

For he has always longed for big horns like Edward Chocolate has on his head.

But instead, his little horns, just make him want to go to bed.

Embarrassed, with cheeks the colour of crimson red.

For at night-time Edward Chocolate plays silly games.

Whilst Bertie Boo Boo ends up being called terrible names.

Night-time came once again, and Bertie Boo Boo braced himself for an unfair game.

Where he most certainly would be called an unpleasant name.

With his long sharp horns, Edward Chocolate seized the night.

Giving all the other animals a great big fright.

Kicking out his hooves and giving a misty snort into the cold air.

The terrified farm animals gasped with absolute despair.

The light against the moon, meant Edward Chocolate's shadow became a great big bull.

And to the other animals, he was certainly making a fool.

They started fleeing and running everywhere.

With a gleeful grin, Edward Chocolate announced...

"In this game of shadows, try and beat me if you dare!"

But even in the bright beautiful moonlight glare.

Bertie Boo Boo managed only to look like a little hare.

"Oh why, oh why!" shouted Bertie Boo Boo, "This just isn't fair!"

Just not enough to give any of the other farm animals a scare.

Not even worthy of a frightful stare.

Not even the little door mouse in the corner got a fright.

He was rolling around the ground, in fits of laughter in the dead of the night.

Suddenly a huge shadow appeared in the night, flying as high,
as high as a kite.

A giant hawk with a terrifying squawk.

Edward Chocolate shouted, "It's a fire breathing dragon!"

"Quickly! Let's head for the wagon!"

"My horns are too big, I can't get under!"

Edward Chocolate became stuck, his face like thunder.

With his little horns, Bertie Boo Boo slipped safely beneath.

Hiding from the scary monster with the great big teeth.

Edward Chocolate shouted, "Oh good grief!"

"This really is beyond belief!"

"I wish I had little horns."

"Life would be much simpler with two pointy thorns."

Suddenly it was clear, a fire breathing dragon there was not.

And indeed, there was no reason for all this fraught.

For the wise owl had swooped down in all the commotion.

28

And came forward with this simple notion...

"Always be happy with what you have and with who you are.

Big horns, little horns and everything afar.

We are all a mixture and that is what is best.

Otherwise too many of one thing would certainly become a pest.

It's better to be different from all the rest."

And that very notion, was just the potion to make Bertie Boo Boo's cheeks so very much less red, whilst dramatically reducing the size of Edward Chocolate's head.

And with that, off they went to bed, deciding to be the very best of friends instead, looking forward to the day ahead.

Big horns, little horns, it really doesn't matter in the end.